# How many Fairy Animals books have you collected?

 Chloe the Kitten

 Bella the Bunny

 Paddy the Puppy

 Mia the Mouse

 Hailey the Hedgehog

 Sophie the Squirrel

 Poppy the Pony

 Betsy the Bunny

 Daisy the Deer

 Katie the Kitten

# Katie the Kitten

Lily Small

EGMONT

With special thanks to Anne Marie Ryan

EGMONT

*We bring stories to life*

*Katie the Kitten* first published in Great Britain 2014
by Egmont UK Limited
The Yellow Building, 1 Nicholas Road
London W11 4AN



ISBN 978 1 4052 7509 5

www.egmont.co.uk
www.hothousefiction.com
www.fairyanimals.com

A CIP catalogue record for this title is available from the British Library.

Printed and bound in Great Britain by The CPI Group

58604/3

# Contents

# CHAPTER ONE

# Camp Sunshine

It was dawn in Misty Wood.
The sun was just starting to rise,
painting the sky with beautiful
stripes of rosy pink and purple.
Katie the Kitten lay on her mossy

bed, listening to birds chirping in the fir tree overhead. Their sweet songs usually woke Katie up, but today she was awake long before the birds started to sing.

Katie jumped out of bed and arched her back, stretching her

glittering blue and golden wings. She glanced at her reflection in a little pool of dew. Then she licked her velvety paws and smoothed down her fluffy white and ginger fur. Katie wanted to look her very best today.

'Good morning,' Mum purred from the other side of their home in the roots of the fir tree. 'Would you like a honey and berry muffin?'

Honey and berry muffins were Katie's favourite breakfast, but this morning she was too excited to eat. It felt like she had a family of butterflies inside her tummy! Katie nibbled a few bites, and then brushed the crumbs off her whiskers. Padding over to a

toadstool, she picked up a little basket resting on top. It was made from woven flower stems.

Most mornings, Katie used her basket to collect water from Dewdrop Spring. Like all the fairy animals of Misty Wood, Katie had a very special job to do. Cobweb Kittens like Katie decorated the cobwebs of Misty Wood with dewdrops so they sparkled in the morning light.

But today Katie was using her basket for something else. She was packing for summer camp!

Every year, the older fairy animal children were invited to spend a weekend at Camp Sunshine. It was the first time Katie was old enough to go! She'd heard loads about camp from the other Cobweb Kittens. There were teams, and challenges, and prizes to win. It sounded like so much

fun – and best of all, her friends Connie and Chloe were going too!

Katie had never spent the night away from home before. She suddenly worried that she might feel homesick at bedtime. Then she had an idea. She went outside and fluttered her wings, heading from tree to tree until she spotted what she was looking for. Stretched between two branches of a tree was a lacy spider's web.

Katie carefully took the cobweb down and folded it neatly. Now she had something to remind her of home.

'It's almost time to go!' Katie's mum called up to her.

Katie fluttered down to where her mother was waiting.

'Do you have any space left in your basket?' Mum asked.

Katie nodded, holding it up.

Mum popped a few muffins

into the basket and twitched her tail playfully. 'I know you're too excited to eat now, but you might get hungry later on.'

It was finally time to set off.

Katie and her mum fluttered their wings and rose into the air.

Below them, Misty Wood stretched out like a glorious paint palette, its colours shining in the morning light. Everywhere they passed, fairy animals were busy working to make the wood a beautiful place to live.

In Honeydew Meadow, Bud Bunnies were hopping into the sunlight, ready to nudge open

the buds of the yellow buttercups. Nearby in the Heart of Misty Wood, Bark Badgers were carving beautiful designs on the tree trunks. Holly Hamsters were nibbling patterns into holly leaves, and Moss Mice were shaping mossy cushions with their paws.

As they flew over Dewdrop Spring, Katie could see the Cobweb Kittens filling their baskets. They laughed as they

dove in and out of the glittering fountain, catching dewdrops that twinkled like diamonds.

The grown-up Cobweb Kittens waved to Katie and called, 'Have fun at camp!'

Katie waved back, but she flew higher in the air to avoid the dazzling jets of water. Although Katie loved making cobwebs sparkle, she wasn't very keen on getting splashed. You see, Katie

had a secret. It was such a big secret that not even her very best friends knew about it. She was scared of water!

They flew a bit further, past a little waterfall and over a glade of trees, and then Katie's mum said, 'Here we are!'

Just ahead of them was Moonshine Pond, shimmering with pearly light. Lilypads dappled the water's surface, and long, fuzzy

cattails and pretty blue irises grew all around the pond.

'But this is Moonshine Pond,' Katie said, confused. From the name, she'd guessed that Camp Sunshine was in a sunny meadow. Oh dear – this wasn't very good at all.

'The camp is just there, by the bank,' said Mum. She pointed towards a colourful row of tents tucked back from the water's edge.

As Katie got closer, she saw that the tents were woven from reeds, and each one was decorated with a different flower. Glossy red poppies, bright yellow daffodils, pretty bluebells and snowy-white lilies, all sweetly perfuming the air.

The camp looked lovely, but Katie felt scared. What if water from the pond splashed her? Or even worse – what if the campers had to go swimming?

'Actually, I think I'd rather stay home,' she fretted.

'Don't be silly,' her mum said. 'You'll have a brilliant time.'

As Katie and her mum landed on the banks of the pond, young fairy animals were playing everywhere. Two Pollen Puppies were wrestling on the ground, while a fluffy Bud Bunny played chase with a group of tiny Moss Mice. A small cluster of Dream

Deer and Hedgerow Hedgehogs stood giggling together.

Katie looked around nervously, but she couldn't see her Cobweb Kitten friends anywhere. Everyone else seemed to have made new friends already.

She gulped. First there was the pond, and now Katie was on her own. The butterflies in her tummy returned, but this time they were flying loop-the-loops!

CHAPTER TWO

# Acorn Team

A beautiful, pale yellow Petal Pony trotted over to Katie, her shimmering blue wings open wide. 'Welcome to Camp Sunshine!' she said. 'Is it your first time here?'

Katie nodded shyly.

'I'm Poppy,' the pony said, flicking her silky mane out of her kind eyes. 'I came to Camp Sunshine last summer and had so much fun. You're going to love it here! Come and meet everyone.'

Katie looked over at the other fairy animals nervously. Would anyone want to be her friend?

'Are you feeling shy?' Poppy asked her gently.

'A little bit,' Katie admitted.

The pony smiled at Katie. 'That's just how I used to feel,' she said. 'Not too long ago, I was much too shy to talk to anyone.'

But Poppy seemed so friendly and brave. 'What did you do?' Katie asked.

'I learned that if you're kind, everyone will want to be your friend,' Poppy said. 'And camp is a great place to make new friends.'

Katie suddenly felt much better. If Poppy could make new friends, then so could she!

Katie turned to her mum. 'I'll miss you,' she meowed, burying her face in her mum's ginger fur.

Mum nuzzled Katie's nose and said, 'I know you'll have a wonderful time, my brave girl.' Then she fluttered her wings and set off for home.

Katie and Poppy flew over to the crowd of campers, who had begun to form a circle. Two Stardust Squirrels were also arriving, their bushy tails leaving a shimmering trail of stardust behind them.

'Hurry up, Sally,' the older squirrel called to the younger one, who was scurrying after her. Then she squealed, 'Hi Poppy! Come and sit next to me.' She turned to her younger sister. 'Stay here, Sally. I'm going to play with my friends.'

The squirrel called Sally sat down next to Katie. A Bud Bunny with soft white fur and spots the colour of conkers hopped over and

sat down on Katie's other side. Her whiskers were trembling, which made Katie think that she might be feeling a bit nervous, too.

Plucking up all her courage, Katie said, 'Hello. I'm Katie. Is this your first time at Camp Sunshine?'

The Bud Bunny nodded. 'I'm Bonnie.' Then she added in a whisper, 'I was so nervous about coming here that I couldn't eat any clover this morning!'

Katie smiled and held out her basket. 'Would you like a honey and berry muffin?'

Bonnie took one and started nibbling. Her purple eyes lit up. 'Yummy scrummy in my tummy!'

Katie giggled. She liked Bonnie. Poppy and her mum were right – it was easy to make new friends when you were kind! Katie asked the Stardust Squirrel on her other side if she'd like a muffin too.

'Thanks,' the squirrel said, helping herself. 'I'm Sally. My big sister Suzy came to camp last summer, so I can tell you everything you need to know.'

But before Katie and Bonnie could ask her any questions, a Bark Badger made his way into the middle of the circle and held up a strong, black paw for silence. The campers stopped chattering and listened with respect, for Bark Badgers were very kind and wise.

'Welcome to Camp Sunshine,' the Bark Badger said. 'I'm Barry, the camp leader. We have a very exciting weekend planned for you.'

He smiled kindly at the campers. 'But first, let's sing our welcome song. Can the campers who've been here before help me teach the others?'

'Oooh – I know this song already,' Sally whispered to Katie and Bonnie. 'My sister taught me.'

Barry cleared his throat and began to sing in a deep voice. Poppy, Suzy and the other older campers chimed in loudly, and

before long everyone else joined in.

'*We love it at Camp Sunshine*

*Where the days are long and fine.*

*We have fun in the summer sun,*

*Welcome, welcome, everyone!*'

When they'd finished singing, Barry said, 'Over the next two days you'll be working in teams.'

*I hope I'm on the same team as Connie or Chloe*, thought Katie, waving to her Cobweb Kitten friends. She'd finally spotted them

sitting across the circle.

'This weekend is all about making *new* friends,' continued Barry. 'So we've put you all in teams with different fairy animals.'

Excited chatter broke out. Then Barry picked up a piece of bark carved with names and read out the teams. Poppy the Petal Pony was in Pinecone Team. Chloe was put on Chestnut Team, and Connie on Buttercup Team.

More teams were called, but Katie wasn't on any of them. Had the Bark Badger forgotten her?

'And last, but not least, we have Acorn Team,' Barry said. 'Petey, Bonnie, Sally and Katie.'

Katie and Bonnie looked at each other in delight. They were on the same team! Katie's tail twitched happily, and Bonnie hopped with excitement.

A brown puppy bounded over and somersaulted to a halt in front of them. Scrambling onto his white paws, he gave a cheerful salute and barked, 'Petey the Pollen Puppy reporting for Acorn Team duty!'

Sally the Stardust Squirrel fluffed out her tail. 'The first thing we need to do is pick our tents,' she said. 'Follow me, girls!'

Katie and Bonnie scampered after her towards the tents.

'How about this one?' Bonnie suggested, pointing at a tent with delicate sprigs of lavender.

'No, this one's much better,' said Sally, hopping over to a tent covered with garlands of bright

orange lilies. Without waiting for a reply from the others, she pushed through the ferns that made the tent's door flap.

Katie and Bonnie followed her inside. As she looked around, Katie gasped. The beds were mossy cushions, just like hers at home. But these cushions were stacked on a frame made out of sticks – one on top of the other!

'I'll have this one!' cried Sally,

fluttering up to the highest cushion and wrapping her fluffy tail around her like a blanket.

Katie chose the bottom bed. She padded over and set down her basket. Then she took out her

cobweb and spread it carefully over her moss cushion.

'What's that?' Sally asked, looking down and frowning.

'It's a cobweb,' explained Katie. 'To remind me of home.'

'I think it's pretty,' Bonnie said.

'We don't need a boring old cobweb to make this tent pretty!' cried Sally. 'I've got a much better idea.' She leaped down from the top bed and spun around in

circles. Her tail shook out a flurry of stardust, making the whole tent shimmer. It did look very pretty but Katie couldn't help feeling a little hurt. She didn't think that cobwebs were boring at all.

Just then, Poppy poked her head around their door flap. 'Don't get too comfy, girls,' she said, laughing when she saw them in their beds. 'The first game is about to begin!'

## CHAPTER THREE

# Woodland Treasure Hunt

Katie and her teammates scampered outside. Petey, who was sharing a tent with a Dream Deer and a Hedgerow Hedgehog,

was waiting for them. Together, Acorn Team made their way over to Barry.

'The first fun activity is a Woodland Treasure Hunt,' he told the campers. 'It's a great test of speed and teamwork. Each team must find five different woodland treasures. The first team to return with all five will be the winner.'

Barry handed Katie a piece of bark with their instructions. Petey,

Bonnie and Sally huddled around.

'We need to find an oak leaf and a twig,' Katie said, pointing at the beautiful pictures Barry had carved with his sharp claws.

'Ooh! And some moss and a daisy,' Bonnie said.

'And a big stone too,' Petey added.

Katie was relieved that they didn't have to bring back any dewdrops from Dewdrop Spring.

'Easy peasy summer breezy,' Sally said. 'I know where to find all those things!'

Katie glanced at the other teams, who were studying their lists and murmuring quietly. 'Maybe we should make a plan first,' she suggested shyly.

But Sally was too busy jumping up and down and cheering. 'We are Acorn Team, so shake your furry tail! We are Acorn

Team and we will never fail!'

Petey's tail wagged so fast it looked like a blur! Bonnie was hopping up and down, too.

Then Barry clapped his hands and called, 'Have fun and remember to work together.' He tooted loudly on a reed flute and the Woodland Treasure hunt began!

'Shall I get my basket?' Katie asked the others. 'It might be handy for carrying our treasures.'

'There's no time for that,' cried Sally. 'Let's go!' She opened her wings and flew up into the air. Petey and Bonnie followed after her, their wings sparkling like rainbows.

Not wanting to be left behind, Katie beat her wings as quickly as she could. 'Where should we go first?' she asked breathlessly.

'To the Heart of Misty Wood, of course,' ordered Sally. 'That's where I gather acorns. There are lots of oak trees there.'

The midday sun warmed their backs as they flew to the very centre of Misty Wood. Trees spread out beneath them like a sea of

green. Katie and her new friends fluttered down to the ground.

It was much cooler here, deep in the woods. The leaves overhead rustled in the breeze.

'This is lovely,' Petey panted, rolling around on the soft ground.

'We don't have time to play,' said Sally bossily. 'We need to find an oak leaf.'

'I see one!' cried Bonnie, hopping over to a big tree. She

came back waving a green leaf.

'Yippee!' called Katie. 'We've got the first treasure on our list!'

Petey ran into the woods for a moment, and came back with a twig in his mouth. He dropped it at their feet with a flourish. 'Here's the second treasure!'

'Hooray!' Katie and Bonnie cried together.

'I've spotted something too,' Sally said. She scampered over

to the oak tree's trunk, where its thick, twisty roots grew out of the damp soil. She scooped something up in her paws, and came back holding a velvety pile of moss. 'That's the third thing,' she said proudly.

'So what's next?' Petey asked.

Katie checked. 'A daisy.'

'I know where there are lots of daisies,' the Pollen Puppy yelped. 'Just follow me!'

Team Acorn rose into the air again. As they flew over Moonshine Pond, Katie glimpsed the colourful row of tents. None of the other teams had returned yet.

'Hurry, team!' cried Sally.

The Golden Meadow stretched in front of them, its green grass dotted with yellow buttercups and dandelions.

Petey dived down and tumbled into a bed of dandelion

clocks, scattering fluffy white seeds everywhere. 'Whee!'

The long green grass tickled Katie's tummy as she landed on the meadow. Nearby, a group of Pollen Puppies were frolicking, wagging their tails and sending up clouds and clouds of fluffy pollen so that new flowers could grow.

'Hi, everyone!' Petey called to the Pollen Puppies. 'Have you seen any daisies?'

A white Pollen Puppy with a black patch over one eye pointed across the meadow. 'Try over there, just past that patch of clover.'

Katie and the others dashed across the meadow after Petey, whose long ears streamed out

behind him. Then he came to a sudden stop and they all tumbled over him into the grass.

'Oops-a-daisy,' joked Petey.

Katie stood up, laughing. They were surrounded by green stalks topped with small, round buds.

'Oh, no,' Petey said, his laughter turning to dismay. 'The daisies haven't bloomed yet.'

*Oh dear*, thought Katie, biting her lip. Sally looked *very* annoyed.

'I'm sorry,' whimpered Petey. 'I really thought we'd find a daisy here.'

'You've forgotten that there's a Bud Bunny on your team,' Bonnie reminded him. Hopping over to the daisy buds, she nudged them gently with her twitching nose.

'Ta da!' she said. As if by magic, the buds started to unfold, one white petal at a time. Then the flowers lifted their yellow faces up

to the sun and bobbed joyfully in the breeze.

'Wow!' Katie breathed.

'It's just what we Bud Bunnies do,' Bonnie said modestly. Then she picked a daisy and tucked it behind her long, silky ear. 'What's the last treasure we need to find?'

'A big stone,' Katie replied.

Everyone thought hard. Where, oh where, could they find a big stone?

'I've got it!' cried Katie. 'There are lots of big stones around Crystal Cave.'

'That's not far from here,' said Petey. With a flurry of beating wings, the fairy animals flew towards the Crystal Cave. Soon Katie could see the crystals inside twinkling like fairy lights.

'Katie was right!' shouted Petey. 'There are lots of big stones.'

The fairy animals landed just

outside the cave. Grunting with effort, Petey picked up a big stone. 'If you take the twig, Katie, I'll carry this.'

But when Petey fluttered his wings, nothing happened. He tried again, beating his wings harder. Still he stayed on the ground.

'What's wrong?' Sally asked, frowning.

'The stone's too heavy,' Petey gasped. 'I can't fly with it.'

'Let me try,' Sally said. 'I'm very strong.' She picked up the stone and fluttered her wings – but it weighed her down too.

'If only we'd brought Katie's basket along,' Bonnie said sadly. 'We could all help carry it.'

That gave Katie an idea. Without stopping to explain, she dashed into Crystal Cave. It was dark and spooky inside. Katie felt along the rough walls until she

found something soft and silky. Gathering it up, she ran back towards the sunlight.

'A cobweb?' said Sally rudely, when she saw what Katie was holding. 'How's that going to help?'

'Cobwebs look delicate, but they're actually very strong,' Katie explained. She spread the cobweb on the ground and placed the stone right in the middle. Then she laid the leaf, the twig and the moss next

to it. 'If we each take one corner of the web, we should be able to fly our treasures back to camp.'

Everyone picked up a corner. 'On my count,' Katie said. 'One . . . two . . . THREE!'

The fairy animals fluttered their wings furiously and rose into the air, lifting the cobweb along with them.

Katie held her breath. Would the cobweb hold?

It sagged in the middle, but the web held strong as they flew with their treasures back to Camp Sunshine. They landed on the banks of the pond and then sprawled on the ground, panting.

'Well done, Acorn Team,' said Barry as he came over to greet them. 'What a clever way to carry your treasures.'

'Did we win?' Sally asked him breathlessly.

'I'm afraid not,' Barry said kindly. He nodded at the pond, where Suzy, Connie and two other fairy animals were splashing in the water. Team Buttercup had won the treasure hunt!

# CHAPTER FOUR
# Show Time

'I expect you're hot after all that hard work,' Barry said, seeing the disappointment on Acorn Team's faces. 'So why don't you cool off with a dip in Moonshine Pond?'

'Come for a swim, Sally,' her sister called. 'The water's lovely!'

'Time for a doggy paddle!' barked Petey, bounding towards the pond.

'Last one in is a stinky toadstool!' Sally cried, chasing after him. Soon most of the campers were splashing in the water. But Katie hung back.

'Don't you want to go swimming?' Bonnie asked her.

Katie didn't want to tell Bonnie her secret. Her new friend seemed kind, but Katie was afraid she'd laugh. It was silly for a Cobweb Kitten to be scared of water!

Katie looked over at the other campers playing in the water. Sally and her sister were floating on their backs, their tails spread underneath them like fluffy rafts.

Poppy the Petal Pony was letting a little Moss Mouse and a Holly Hamster slide down her long neck and splash into the water. Petey was clowning around, wearing a water lily on his head. Everyone was having so much fun. But even the thought of dipping her paw in the water made the butterflies in Katie's tummy come back.

'Er . . . my tummy hurts a bit,' Katie said.

'You poor thing!' Bonnie exclaimed. 'I'll keep you company.'

Katie and Bonnie stretched out under a weeping willow tree. They gazed up at the blue sky dotted with clouds as white and fluffy as Bonnie's tail.

'Why don't we look for pictures in the clouds?' Bonnie suggested. She pointed her paw up at the sky. 'See! There's a fish.'

Katie tilted her head and

squinted at the cloud. It *did* look like a fish. What a fun game! She stared up at the sky, and suddenly saw lots of interesting shapes. 'Ooh! That one looks like

a pinecone. And that one looks like a hedgehog balancing on a toadstool.'

The rest of the afternoon flew by. When the sun had dipped lower in the sky, Barry called the campers over for their dinner.

Katie's eyes grew wide when she saw the feast laid out on a big old tree stump. There was wild mushroom medley, watercress salad, a big pile of hazelnuts,

and heaps of plump, juicy blackberries. It all looked wonderful!

Katie and Bonnie filled their acorn bowls to the brim and sat down with Petey and Sally around a toadstool table. Mmm – it tasted delicious! Katie finished every bite of her dinner, and still had room for a big bowl of blackberries.

A full moon shimmered overhead. Stars twinkled against a velvet sky, and fireflies swirled

through the night air like sparklers. Owls hooted softly and crickets chirped, singing Misty Wood to sleep with their lullabies. But the campers weren't ready for bed yet.

'Now for our next activity! We're going to put on a talent show,' Barry said. 'Each team will work together on an act, and the team that gets the loudest applause will win.'

Acorn Team huddled together to plan their act.

'I can dance!' said Bonnie.

'And I can juggle,' Petey said, picking up three hazelnuts and starting to juggle them.

Sally plucked the hazelnuts out of the air and popped them in her mouth. 'I've got a better idea,' she said. 'We'll put on a play.'

'What will it be about?' asked Katie.

Sally thought for a moment. 'It will be about a beautiful and clever Stardust Squirrel who dances in the moonlight. I'll play the Stardust Squirrel, of course.'

'Who will the rest of us be?' asked Bonnie, disappointed.

'Hmm,' said Sally. 'Katie and Bonnie, you two can be trees. And Petey, you can be . . . the moon.'

They started practising their play. Sally told everyone where to

stand and what to do. Then, as she pranced about and said her lines, Katie and Bonnie waved branches in the air, pretending to be trees. Katie swayed and tried to look tree-like, but wished she had a bigger part.

Petey was supposed to stand still and look serious, but he kept humming a lively tune and chasing his tail. *'Clap your paws and make a sound,'* Petey sang

under his breath. '*Find a partner and spin them round.*'

'Stop it, Petey!' Sally said crossly. 'We won't win if you don't do what I tell you.'

'But it's boring,' whined Petey. 'You're the only one who gets to do anything interesting.'

'Maybe we should try something different,' suggested Bonnie.

'Like what?' sulked Sally.

'I know!' said Katie. 'We can

all perform Petey's song together.'

Even Sally had to agree it was a good idea. They had just enough time for a quick rehearsal before Barry called everyone back together. It was showtime!

Chestnut Team was the first to perform. They had written a sweet poem about Camp Sunshine and recited it together. After that, Buttercup Team did a comedy routine, with every team member

telling a funny joke. Katie laughed so hard that her sides ached.

Pinecone Team was on next. They did a breathtaking flying display, turning loop-the-loops and zooming around upside-down. For their finale, they all flew in a perfect V-shaped formation with Poppy the Petal Pony at the centre. Katie thought she looked beautiful, as her blue wings glittered in the moonlight and her

silky tail fluttered in the breeze. When Pinecone Team finished with dramatic nosedives to the ground, the applause was deafening.

After a few more acts, it was finally Acorn Team's turn. Katie squeezed Bonnie's paw for good luck as they nervously waited for the music to begin.

Petey started them off, beating out a rhythm on an acorn drum. Then Sally joined in, playing a

lively tune on reed pipes. Katie and Bonnie danced in time to the music as they all sang Petey's song:

*'Clap your paws and make a sound,*
*Find a partner and spin them round.*
*All the fairy animals sing along now –*
*Doo-bee-doo, then BOW-WOW-WOW!'*

Katie and Bonnie whirled round faster and faster. Every time it came to the chorus, they bowed to each other and spun round the opposite way. The audience

clapped along happily to the music.

When the song was over, Acorn Team bowed and basked in the applause. Katie could see her friends Connie and Chloe cheering loudly. The crowd had

clearly enjoyed their act, but was it enough to win?

Katie held her breath as Barry read out the results.

'It was close,' he said. 'Acorn Team's song got a very loud cheer, but the winner of the talent show is . . . Pinecone Team!'

'Oh conkers and cobwebs,' muttered Sally. 'Second again.'

Katie shrugged and smiled at her team. 'I still had fun.'

As Poppy and her team proudly took another bow, a pale figure drifted overhead, casting a long shadow over the performers.

Katie glanced up. 'What's *that*?' she asked, pointing at the spooky shape.

'I don't know,' Bonnie whispered nervously.

'Eek!' shrieked Sally. 'It's a ghost!'

CHAPTER FIVE

# Morning Glory

Katie gasped as the spooky figure hovered in the air. Could it really be a ghost? She and Bonnie and Sally clung to each other in fright.

But then Suzy laughed. 'Don't

be so silly,' she said. 'It's just a Moonbeam Mole.'

Katie peeped past Bonnie and saw a Moonbeam Mole flying over the pond. He tipped out his net and scattered glittering moonbeams over the water. They bobbed on the surface, making gleaming, pearly ripples. It was lovely!

The campers called hello to the Moonbeam Mole, who gave them a friendly wave in return.

Then he flew away again, his silvery wings twinkling.

'If the Moonbeam Moles have woken up and started their work, it must be time for us to go to bed,' Barry said. 'Come on, kids.'

'But I'm not even sleepy!' Petey protested with a big yawn.

As the pond's dark water shimmered in the moonlight, Katie headed back to the tent with Bonnie and Sally. Her new friends fluttered up to their beds, and Katie curled up on her mossy cushion, snuggling under her cobweb blanket.

'Nighty-night,' Sally called softly from the top bed.

'Sleep tight,' whispered Bonnie from the middle bed.

But Katie fell fast asleep before she could even reply.

Katie was having a lovely dream about dancing under a starry sky with a Moonbeam Mole. They were scattering moonbeams all over Misty Wood, twirling faster and faster until –

'Wakey, wakey, sleepyhead,'

called Sally. 'Time to rise and shine.'

Katie opened her eyes and looked around the tent. Where was she? Then she smiled. It was her second day at Camp Sunshine!

Katie licked her paws and quickly washed her face. Then she and the girls stepped out of their tent into the glorious early-morning sunshine. They joined Petey and the other campers for a

tasty breakfast of seedy loaf and rosehip jam washed down with cups of acorn milk.

'I hope you all slept well,' Barry said with a smile. 'Today each team will be making something very special.'

'I wonder what it will be,' Bonnie said.

'I bet we'll be weaving baskets,' Petey guessed. 'Or maybe Barry will teach us wood carving.

You can make a picture of me if you like!' He stood on his hind legs, wagged his tail and stuck out his long pink tongue.

Katie and Bonnie giggled. Petey was *so* funny!

'Don't be silly,' Sally said, rolling her eyes. 'We're camping, so I'm sure we'll be making tents. My sister went here *last* year, remember.'

But Sally and Petey were both

wrong. After breakfast, Barry gathered the campers by the side of the pond. 'Today you'll be making boats,' he revealed.

'Yay!' shouted Petey. 'I've always wanted to go sailing!' He danced a wild sailor's jig.

But Katie suddenly felt very cold. Oh, no! She definitely did *not* want to go sailing!

But to her relief, Barry explained that they wouldn't be

sailing the boats themselves. 'Each team will make a model boat, and at the end of the day you'll race them on the pond,' he said.

Katie let out a breath. She could be brave enough to go *near* the pond, as long as she didn't have to go *on* it!

'Right, let's get started,' said Sally, rubbing her paws together. 'Acorn Team has *got* to win today!'

'Maybe we should plan our

boat first,' Katie said. She picked up a twig and started sketching a boat in the thick, oozy mud at the edge of the pond.

'That's a waste of time,' Sally said impatiently. 'I already know how to make a boat. Come on!'

'Aye, aye captain,' Petey said, and the rest of the team followed the trail of sparkling stardust from Sally's tail.

Katie followed too, but Sally's

bossiness *was* starting to annoy her a bit.

Sally led her teammates to a grove of trees. 'Find as many sticks as you can,' she ordered them.

Bonnie and Katie scampered to and fro, gathering up twigs in their paws. Petey dragged bigger sticks over in his mouth.

Soon, there was a big pile by Sally's feet. She started to weave the sticks and twigs together into

the shape of a boat. The others tried to help, but Sally shooed them away. 'Fetch me some nice, long grass,' she said.

'Fetch this, fetch that,' Petey grumbled as they plucked the

longest blades of grass they could find.

'I thought puppies liked to play fetch,' Katie joked, but secretly she was glad she wasn't the only one who thought Sally was being bossy.

When they returned with the grass, Sally used it to tie the twigs together. Katie looked on, wishing she could help.

'There! It's done,' Sally

announced, sounding pleased with herself. 'Now let's test it out.'

Katie and her team carried the boat back to Moonshine Pond. It was surprisingly heavy.

With a big heave, Sally pushed the boat into the water. But instead of sailing away, it just bobbed on the surface.

'Why isn't it moving?' Sally muttered.

'Er, it *is* moving, Sally,' Petey

said. 'Just not the way we want it.'

They looked on in horror. The boat was slowly sinking into the pond! Down, down, down it went, until finally it vanished underwater. A few bubbles floated to the surface and then – *pop!* – they were gone too.

'Oh no!' Sally wailed.

'Don't worry,' Bonnie said, giving Sally a hug. 'We have plenty of time to make another boat.'

'And we'll *all* help,' Katie said, smiling at Petey.

This time, Acorn Team sat by the pond and planned their boat before they started building it.

'The way Sally tied the twigs together was very clever,' said Katie.

'But maybe it should be lighter,' suggested Bonnie.

They all gathered more twigs. This time Sally collected lots

too, and they soon had plenty. Everyone helped to build the boat, trying out different designs until they decided on the best shape.

'I've got an idea,' Petey said. He splashed into the pond and paddled over to a cluster of lilypads. Petey put the lilypad on his head and swam back to shore with it flopping into his eyes.

*Is Petey being silly again*? Katie wondered.

Sloshing out of the water, Petey carefully pressed the big, round lilypad into the boat. 'This will be a waterproof lining,' he explained.

'Clever!' Katie said, helping to smooth it down.

'Now we need a mast,' said Bonnie.

Petey dragged a long stick over, and Sally tied it to the middle of the boat. Bonnie picked

a morning glory vine and wound it around the mast. Twitching her nose against the vine, she nudged its flowers open until the mast was wreathed in blue blossoms.

But the boat still needed a sail. Katie had an idea. 'I'll be right back!'

She quickly flew to her tent and scooped up her lacy cobweb. Then she flew back to the boat and carefully tied it to the mast.

There were still drops of water glistening on the lilypad lining, so Katie sprinkled them onto the sail as a finishing touch.

Then she and the others stepped back to admire their boat. It was sleek but sturdy. The lacy cobweb sail billowed gently in the breeze and the drops of water twinkled like crystals in the sunshine.

'It's beautiful!' breathed Katie.

'Let's go and test it out,' Petey suggested.

But it was too late. The other teams had all gathered around Barry. The race was about to begin!

CHAPTER SIX

# The Boat Race

Acorn Team carefully carried their beautiful boat to the pond. A light breeze ruffled the sparkling water. It was a perfect day for a boat race!

The other teams' boats were wonderful. Poppy's Pinecone Team had obviously been inspired by their name. They'd built their boat from fir cones glued together with sticky pinesap.

Chestnut Team had made their boat from silvery birch bark. Its green sail was a quilt of leaves, daintily stitched together with grass.

Buttercup Team's boat had

the most unusual design. Two small logs floated on the water, and a raft made from sticks rested between them.

Still, Katie thought that Acorn Team's was the most beautiful by

far. She crossed her paws for luck.

Barry licked his paw and held it up to see what way the wind was blowing. 'Ahoy there, campers! On my signal, you'll launch your ships.' He pointed his paw to the

bank of the pond beneath the willow tree. 'The first boat to land on the other side of the pond will be the winner.'

The teams readied their boats. Petey tinkered with the lining and Katie made sure the cobweb sail was still firmly attached. The cobweb was as light as a feather, but Team Acorn knew how strong it really was.

'We've just got to win,' Sally

said. She shook her tail and gave the boat a sprinkling of stardust for luck.

Katie hoped the lucky stardust would work – and that their boat wouldn't sink this time. If only they'd been able to test it . . .

'Anchor's aweigh!' cried Barry, and the race was on!

Bonnie, Petey, and Sally waded into the pond, but Katie hung back. She didn't want to get

too close to the water. She watched anxiously as her friends gave the boat a gentle push.

The beautiful boat bobbed in place for a moment. Katie held her breath. Would it float?

Yes! It sailed away, gliding over the rippling water, and quickly took the lead.

'Yay!' Sally cried. 'Let's go to the finish line so we can watch it win!'

Katie hesitated. What if the boat got into trouble and they weren't there to help? 'Shouldn't we wait a bit?' she said.

'Don't be such a worrywart,' Sally said. 'Come on, we don't want to miss the finish!'

Sally took off across Moonshine Pond. Bonnie and Petey flitted after her. All around Katie, excited fairy animals were making their way to the other side.

Katie was about to follow when she noticed that their boat had tilted to the side and changed its course. It was heading straight towards a patch of reeds!

'Wait!' she cried, but the others were already off.

Katie watched in horror as their lovely boat sailed right into the reeds. Soon, it was hopelessly tangled in the long, marshy grasses.

In the distance, Katie could see Bonnie, Sally and Petey heading to the finishing line. But their boat would never get there if it stayed stuck! Katie knew she couldn't let that happen.

Gathering all her courage, she opened her wings and rose into the air. She flew to the patch of reeds, and hovered over the boat. Fluttering her wings furiously so that she wouldn't fall in the water,

Katie reached down and gave the boat a nudge, but it didn't move. She pushed it again, harder this time, trying not to get wet. Still the boat was stuck fast.

By now, the other boats were already halfway across the pond.

'Help!' Katie cried. 'Acorn Team!' But all the fairy animals were at the other side of the pond, and their cheers drowned out Katie's desperate cries.

Katie thought about her teammates waiting for the boat that would never get there. They had worked so hard and this was their last chance to win a prize at Camp Sunshine. As the boat struggled to break free of the reeds, Katie's heart sank.

There was only one thing to do – but was she brave enough to do it?

She took a big gulp of air, and

squeezed her eyes shut. She *could* do it. She had to.

Then she dived into the water!

A moment later, she came spluttering to the surface, her eyes opened wide with surprise. The water felt slippery and . . . *lovely*! Moving the reeds out of the way, she gave the boat a big push and it sailed free.

Katie paddled her paws until she reached the side of the pond.

Then, after clambering out, she flew over to the finishing line.

'Why are you all wet?' Bonnie asked.

'Our boat got tangled in some reeds,' Katie said. 'But I got it out.'

Their boat was moving swiftly across the pond now, its cobweb sail blowing in the wind. It had nearly caught up to the other boats.

'Come on, little boat!' cheered Bonnie.

It cruised past Buttercup Team's boat.

'You can do it!' shrieked Sally.

It glided past Pinecone Team's boat.

'Nearly there!' barked Petey.

But Chestnut Team's boat was just too far ahead. It cruised to the finish line first. Chestnut Team cheered and hugged each other. Moments later, Acorn Team's boat reached the finishing line, in second place once again.

'I'm so sorry,' Sally said, her voice trembling. 'I should have listened to you, Katie. If we'd all been there to help you, we might

have got the boat free sooner and won.' Tears glistened in her eyes. 'I was being bossy again. Just like my big sister always bosses *me* around.'

'It's OK,' Katie said, giving

her a hug. 'We still did really well. You should be proud that we finished second!'

'If it wasn't for your quick thinking, we wouldn't have finished at all,' Sally sniffled.

When all the boats had finished, Barry gathered the campers for the end of camp prize-giving ceremony. 'Have you all had fun?' he asked the campers.

Katie and the other campers

shouted, 'Yes!' and cheered loudly.

First, Barry presented Buttercup Team with the Treasure Hunt award. On a piece of bark he'd carved a beautiful picture of a treasure chest. As Suzy went up with her team to collect the award, Sally cheered the loudest. But Katie could tell how badly her friend had wanted a prize too.

'Don't worry,' she reassured Sally, patting her fluffy back.

'There's always next summer.'

Pinecone Team was given an award carved with stars for winning the Talent Show. Poppy trotted up to collect their prize with the other members of Pinecone Team on her back.

Finally, Chestnut Team bounded up to receive their prize, which was carved with a picture of a boat. Katie clapped her paws together and cheered for all the

winners. It would have been nice to win something, but Katie was just happy to be there. She could hardly believe it was nearly time to go home.

But to her surprise, Barry held up another award.

'And now, for a very special prize,' he announced. 'The Camp Sunshine Team Spirit award goes to four of our newest campers. Over the past two days, this

team has learned how to work together – even when it wasn't easy. Most importantly, they've become good friends and that's what Camp Sunshine is all about! Congratulations . . . Acorn Team!'

Sally leapt up and down, sprinkling glitter from her tail in excitement. Petey ran around in circles and Katie hugged Bonnie tight. Then they all went up to collect a beautiful bark award

carved with a smiling sun and a row of tents.

As the other campers cheered, Katie glowed with pride. Coming to Camp Sunshine was the best thing ever! Not only had she and her new friends won an award, but she wasn't scared of water anymore. She'd never have to worry about Dewdrop Spring again.

Katie sighed happily. It was

the perfect ending to a perfect weekend. Camp Sunshine was even better than she'd dreamed it would be. She'd made so many friends and had so much fun. Katie couldn't wait to come back next summer!

Turn the page for
lots of fun
Misty Wood
activities!

# Spot the difference

The picture on the opposite page is slightly different to this one. Can you circle all the differences?

Hint: there are eight differences in this picture!

Can you find all these words from Katie's story?

| A | C | O | B | W | E | B | B | P | C | T | E | A | M | D |
|---|---|---|---|---|---|---|---|---|---|---|---|---|---|---|
| E | A | D | A | I | S | Y | S | O | N | G | F | H | E | B |
| A | M | B | D | A | C | O | R | N | E | R | A | E | A | O |
| O | P | L | I | L | Y | P | A | D | N | O | P | T | E | A |
| D | A | I | M | P | T | R | E | A | S | U | R | E | I | T |

ACORN COBWEB TEAM POND CAMP TREASURE
DAISY SONG BOAT LILYPAD